The Froggies Do NOT Want to Sleep

Adam Gustavson

Charlesbridge

The froggies

do NOT want to sleep.

They want to hOp.

They want to practice
their accordions

and ride their unicycles . . .

. . . and play dress-up.

But they **do not** want to sleep.

They want to go for long drives in the country . . .

. . . and joust

like knights.

They want to dance underwater ballet

and tame ferocious beasties.

They want

to sing opera

while firing themselves
out of cannons.

They are far too busy
    flying their spaceships

and zipping through galaxies,

with strange, alien life-forms.

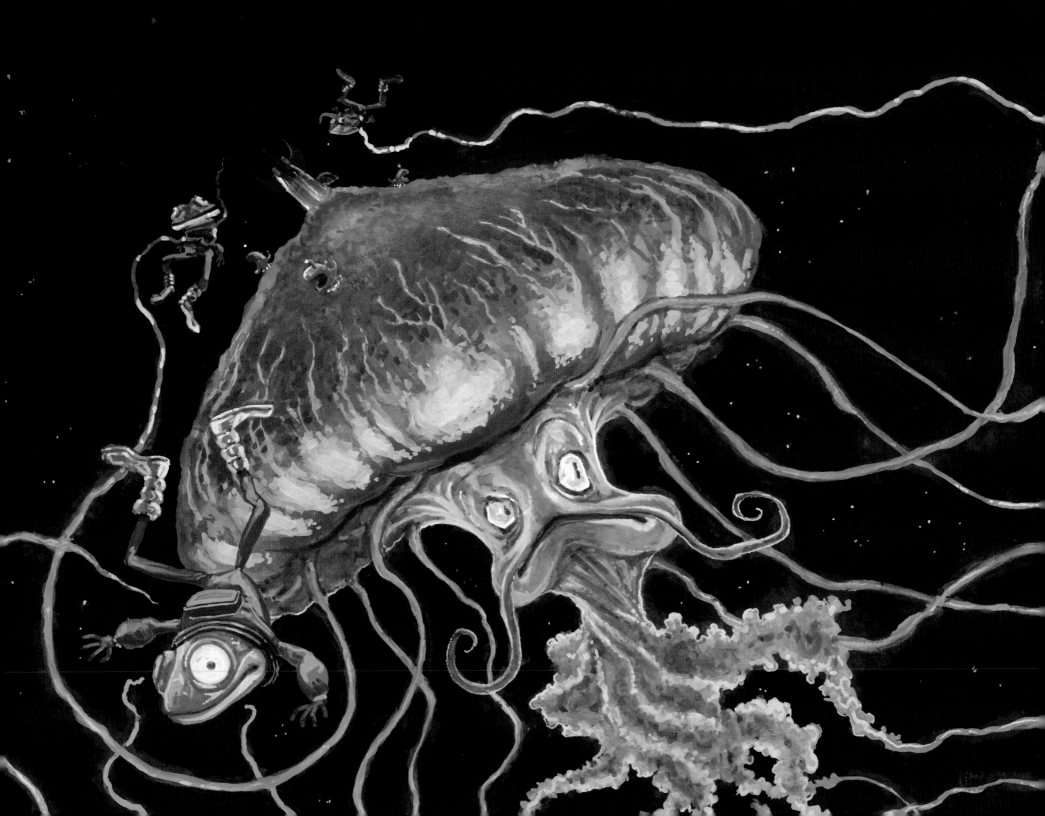

And if a giant jelly-headed
space monster
should wake up and grab them
and squeeeeeze them . . .

. . . and tickle their sides
and their toes
and their bellies . . .

. . . and send them tumbling
through piles
of pillowy clouds,
one thing is certain.

The froggies

do not want . . .

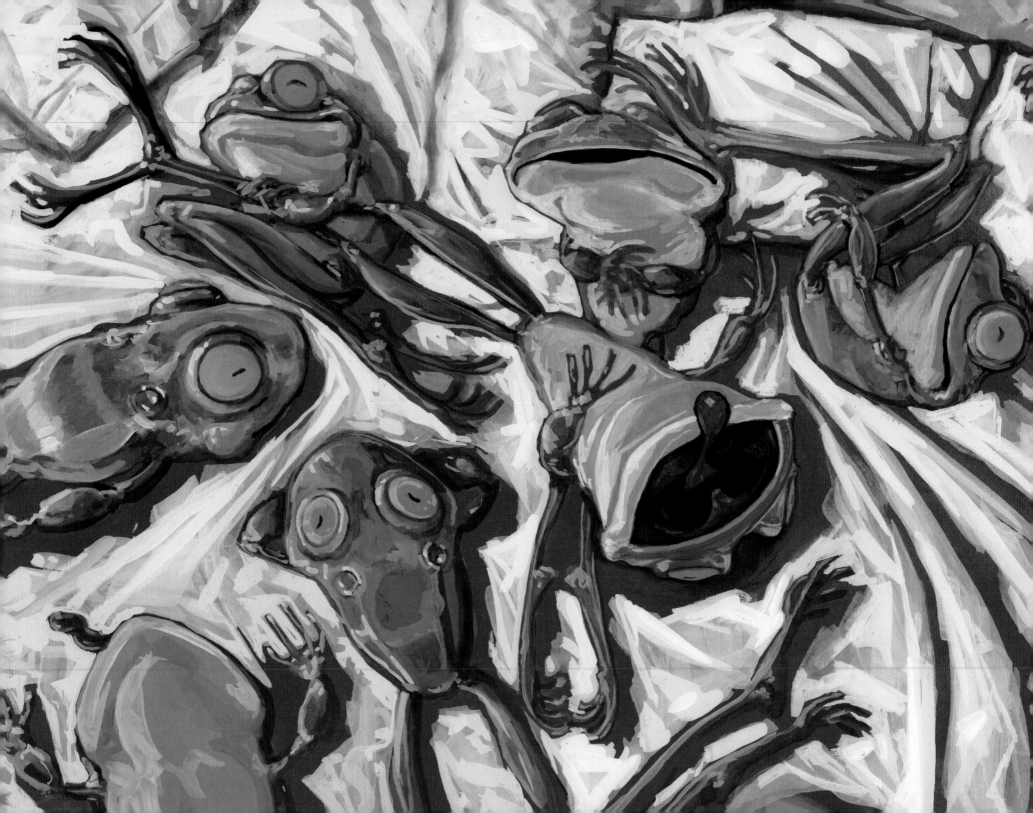

. . . to sleep.

For Denise and the boys—A. G.

Charlesbridge and colophon are registered trademarks of
Charlesbridge Publishing, Inc.

At the time of publication, all URLs printed in this book
were accurate and active. Charlesbridge and the author are not
responsible for the content or accessibility of any website.

Published by Charlesbridge
9 Galen Street
Watertown, MA 02472
(617) 926-0329
www.charlesbridge.com

Library of Congress Cataloging-in-Publication Data
Names: Gustavson, Adam, author, illustrator.
Title: The froggies do not want to sleep / Adam Gustavson.
Description: Watertown, MA: Charlesbridge Publishing, [2021] | Audience:
    Ages 3–7. | Audience: Grades K–1. | Summary: "The froggies do not
    want to sleep and refuse to head to bed; they'd rather play their
    accordions, go for long drives in the country, or sing opera while
    shooting themselves out of cannons"—Provided by publisher.
Identifiers: LCCN 2020017265 (print) | LCCN 2020017266 (ebook) |
    ISBN 9781580895248 (hardcover) | ISBN 9781632898395 (ebook)
Subjects: CYAC: Frogs—Fiction. | Bedtime—Fiction.
Classification: LCC PZ7.1.G883 Fr 2021 (print) | LCC PZ7.1.G883 (ebook) |
    DDC [E]—dc23
LC record available at https://lccn.loc.gov/2020017265
LC ebook record available at https://lccn.loc.gov/2020017266

Printed in China
(hc) 10 9 8 7 6 5 4 3 2 1

Illustrations created in gouache and watercolor on paper, with a teensy
    bit of help from Adobe Photoshop
Display type set in Bureau Grotesque by Adobe Systems Incorporated
Text type set in Berkeley Oldstyle by ITC
Color separations by Colourscan Print Co Pte Ltd, Singapore
Printed by 1010 Printing International Limited in Huizhou,
    Guangdong, China
Production supervision by Jennifer Most Delaney
Designed by Cathleen Schaad